Titles available by Greg James

The Vetala Cycle
The Eyes of the Dead
Shapes in the Mist
Hell's Teeth

Standalone Horror
The Thing Behind the Door
This Darkness Mine
Night Residue
Sevengraves
London Ghost Story
The Clowns Outside

The Age of the Flame Trilogy – YA Fantasy
The Sword of Sighs
The Sceptre of Storms
The Stone of Sorrows

Khale the Wanderer – Grimdark Fantasy
Under A Colder Sun
Lost is the Night

The Chronicles of Willow Grey – YA Fantasy
The Door of Dreams

The Clowns Outside

By Greg James

Acknowledgments

I would like to thank the following people for their help, support and contributions;

Lora Kaleva – for always being there for me.

Emma Audsley – for answering all my questions on coulrophobia and being the perfect (un)willing victim.

Robyn Porter – for being a great friend and helping me undertake the task of rebranding my first run of horror releases.

Ed McNally & Heather Marie Adkins – for being great friends and banterers of the highest order.

The lads of Great British Horror – thanks for listening, as well as offering your advice and support. It means a great deal to me.

My beta-readers and proof-readers – you know who you are and I can't thank you enough ever.

Finally, to all of my friends, fellow authors and fans that I have not mentioned above – thank you for your support.

Dedication

This one is for Emma, Ann, and Dianne.

' ... send in the clowns ... '

Chapter One

Emma Ashley was alone in the house. The boys were away visiting Grandma and Grandad. The house felt very empty without them. She could feel the silence as a weight in the air; aching to be broken by young, high voices – none came and the silence went on with her as its witness. She'd needed this weekend though; a break from the boys. She loved them more than herself but there were times when she felt how much time and space they took up, and how little she had left to herself. She was Mummy now more than she was Emma or Emms.

Jacob was autistic and had his needs; she often thought on how he would live in this world as she watched him sleep; only a scraggy tuft of his dark blonde hair showed from under the duvet as if he were hibernating in there, desperate to keep warm. The world was a cold place, and its people, colder still. She hoped he would be okay because that was all she could do – hope. Liam was a wiry monkey next to Jacob's quiet, reserved gentleness. Maybe he would watch out for Jacob as they grew older. Again, she hoped knowing it was all out of her hands.

In the pressing quiet of the house, Emma looked down at her hands, turned them over and brushed the fingertips against one another. They were a mother's hands and sometimes she couldn't believe they were hers. Mother. Mummy. Emma. Emms. She was all these things and yet sometimes she felt like none of them. She tried not to look but her eyes were drawn to the pale circle of skin at the root of her left ring finger. He was gone now. She'd left him and was starting over again – and she'd needed this weekend alone before taking the first steps along the path ahead.

The old routine was over, and the old path was overrun with bitter weeds. The path ahead couldn't be seen clearly – but a part of her couldn't wait to explore it. Without the boys, she could follow it a little way over the next few days and see where it might lead. There were nerves singing in her fingers and palms. A smile broke out on her face as she left the house and took the first steps along the path of her new life.

*

Emma's walk in the woods was slow-going as her bad leg was playing up; aches and twinges came and went as she trod through the leaves and bracken of a wintering autumn. The trees were dressed only in skins of crumbling bark and stubbled moss. The long fingers of their branches seemed to drag their way across the grey flesh of the afternoon sky; groping at it as a child might when touching its mother's skin. The woods were still with the same hibernating quiet she'd often felt in the boys' bedroom. They'd be getting too old to share a room and bunk beds soon. They were growing up so fast and she did miss them, but she'd missed this as well – being alone with the world in a quiet place. She'd come out here a lot as a teenager and in her twenties; just to listen to the woods. You could feel it if you tried; a sort of breathing, of life all around you yet unseen, just below the surface, out of sight, almost close enough to touch. All you had to do was reach out and it would be there as if it had been waiting for you since before you were born; that's what it felt like out here.

She'd told the boys about the feeling she got in the woods once. Liam had smiled, laughed and clapped his hands at the idea. Jacob had looked afraid and pulled away. Emma didn't sleep well afterwards though and when she went in to check on the boys, she saw Jacob's eyes awake and watching the dark as it moved around him.

In that moment, she'd seen herself in her son's face and remembered being a child in her Mum's old place and the dolls; and the night when she'd felt herself first touched by life's shadow. She went to Jacob at the time, held him, told him it was okay and didn't let go of him until long after he fell back to sleep and the sun had arisen. No shadow came near her son whilst he was in her arms – and that was as it should be.

Today, it was peaceful in the woods and Emma kicked the memory of fear away in a crackling flurry of leaves. Pain stung her leg; a sharp reminder of unwanted frailty. She came to a clearing where some kind soul had erected benches for the weary and sat down. The aches and pains in her leg muscles began to subside. She rubbed her hand over the thigh of her bad leg. When she was little and came home with scabs on her knees or a bump on her head, Mum always stroked her hand over the injury and kissed it better. Emma knew it was the plasters and ointment applied afterwards which made things get better but it always felt like it was really Mum's touch that made the pain go away. She did the same thing when Jacob and Liam banged themselves up and now she was alone, she wished that she could work the same magic on herself. It didn't work like that though. She knew that. Everyone knew that – only a mother can heal a child – and her Mum was long gone. Five years and a bit since the cancer metastasized from lungs to bones. No more kisses better. No more hugs. No more Mum.

Emma blinked a few tears away and tried to brighten her thoughts by looking at the trees, stirring the leaves on the ground with the toes of her trainers, but it didn't work. The thin, black branches were the dead nerves in her leg which the surgeon had cut through. She imagined them lying there, rigid beneath her skin, waiting to dig in like old needles whenever she made the leg work too hard. There was no cure for this and no physiotherapy. The cancer had been cut out but then bad things always come back, Emma thought as her eyes examined the clouds overhead. They'd told her it might not be over. All the pain and dead nerves could be for nothing in the end and the passing clouds today looked like old, bloated tumours.

"What we have is broken," Emma whispered to herself, "but it is all we have."

The boys would learn things like this one day and Emma didn't want that to happen. She wanted them here now so she could hold them so tight that time would stop and that day never came to pass.

Let me have it, she thought, *let all the pain be for me and not them. Do it all to me. Hurt me every day and every night if it must be, just leave them alone. Let them be.*

There was no stopping time though, she knew that.

"Bad things always come back." She said aloud.

It was then Emma realised that she was no longer alone in the clearing. There was a man standing among the trees; swaying on his feet, his shoulders slouched, his head cocked to one side as if listening. He came towards her, scuffing his feet through the dead leaves. He was dressed strangely. In place of the dirty jeans and stained shirt that would've seemed more fitting to someone in his state, there was a clown's outfit. It was torn and tattered but she could see bright, baggy colours showing through the grime. A huge yellow necktie, limp and unwashed, hung around the blotchy scrag of his throat. There was some red smeared on his nose that might have been blood and his face was marked by fading streaks of white greasepaint. Emma's fingers gripped the wood of the bench tightly. She didn't want him anywhere near to her. She hated clowns.

He stopped a few feet away and blinked. His eyes were restless as he opened his mouth and spoke, "Cou-could you let me know the time please?"

Emma looked at him, not wanting to look away. Her phone was in her pocket. He snorted wetly and wiped a sleeve arm across his face, making it ride up past his wrist. He was wearing a watch. He lowered the arm and waited, swaying again.

"Is your watch broken?" Emma asked.

He blinked again, slowly, and picked his nose. Red stained his finger and she still wasn't sure if it was blood or make-up.

Emma kept her eyes on him as she fumbled in her pocket for her phone. He just stood there, rocking on his feet, dressed in that ridiculous outfit. Maybe it was a stag do, she thought, and he's been left behind by his mates. They dressed him up like a prat and dumped him in the woods last night and he's been wandering around, lost and hungover, ever since. He took a stumbling step forward, righted himself, and grinned. Emma moved away from him along the bench, hoping he didn't decide to sit down next to her. He didn't. He carried on standing, swaying drunkenly.

"Time please," he said again, with a far-away, sing-song tone to his voice.

A light breeze blew through the trees, making the baggy trousers, sleeves and bloated rump of his clothes mutter, whisper, and shush.

"It's half four," Emma said quickly, returning her phone to her pocket.

He blinked at her and carried on standing there as if he hadn't heard a thing; swaying in the wind. Her toes were curling in her trainers and she resisted the urge to shut her eyes tight and try to wish him away like she used to wish away the clowns when she was little; the ones that scratched at the bedposts, tickled her feet with their cold hands, and made the shadows dance darkly all night long.

I've not thought about them in years, she thought as she decided to get up and go.

This guy either didn't want her help or was beyond help until he sobered up. She got to her feet and, as she did, he turned around and began to shuffle off through the leaves. He was going away, across the clearing, back into the trees.

He'll be gone soon.

Emma let out a breath. Her bad leg chose that moment to cramp up badly and force her back down onto the bench with a hard gasp. The pain cut through her, making her stomach surge and lunge until she tasted bile at the back of her throat. She closed her eyes against the pain. She didn't cry out and didn't scream; not when Mum died, not when she was told about the botched surgery, not when she left him and all of his bullshit, and not now.

I'm going home.

Leaves shuffled and scuffed over her trainers. Emma opened her eyes. He was back and standing over her this time, smiling a smile as empty as his eyes.

"I have to be somewhere," he said.

She looked at him, unblinking, "Where?"

"I don't have money. I need to be somewhere close by."

He wasn't a drunk, he was a beggar. Emma wanted to tell him to fuck off and leave her alone. There was something wrong with him and she was in pain. She let out a slow breath before she spoke, "I'm sorry. I can't help you. I don't have any cash on me and I can't drive. I can't take you anywhere."

The smile stayed where it was, "I know. We know."

"Who's we?" she said, looking around.

There was no-one else in the trees that she could see.

"You're a nice lady," he said, "if I take my clothes off, will you tell me what you think?"

Emma's tongue went still for a moment and her mouth dried out. "I'm sorry, what did you just say?"

"If I take my clothes off, will you tell me what you think?"

"You're joking."

He went on smiling, his glacial eyes twitching in their sockets. Emma sat up straight and took her phone out, "I want you to go please, now. I'm calling the police."

He just stood there.

"I am doing it."

He didn't move.

"I fucking am."

She dialled 999 and waited. The phone rang, connected and someone picked up.

"Which emergency service please?"

"Police."

"Thank you, just putting you through."

The line clicked and Emma said, "Police?"

"Hello," a voice replied.

"I need someone to come out to my house. Well, near to my house. I'm in the woods."

"We know."

"What?"

She looked at the clown and the smile lingering on his face.

"You're a nice lady. Clever. Funny. Beautiful."

"What the fuck is going on? Is this the police? Is this a joke?"

She was listening to the clown's voice on her phone.

"If I take my clothes off, will you tell me what you think?"

"No, I won't," she said, not believing what was happening.

The smile on the clown's face broadened.

"If you take your clothes off, I'll tell you what I think."

Emma stabbed at her phone with a finger, ending the call, "Jesus Christ."

The clown was still there, still smiling, and he'd taken his penis out.

It was hanging out of his billowing trousers; wrinkled, limp, and pale. He stroked at it with his grotty fingers. "You can touch it," he said, "like we used to touch you with the shadows, Emma."

She lunged to her feet, grabbed at him, and thumped him hard in the chest. *"Leave me the fuck alone!"*

The clown staggered back, caught his heels on the baggy cuffs of his trousers, and lost his balance. His arms flailed wildly as he fell. His legs flew up in the air when he hit the ground as if it were planned. Next, silence and no round of applause.

Emma slowly walked over to him. She'd expected him to take the hint, get up and run away after she hit him, but he wasn't moving. He was spread-eagled on the ground like a clown after a circus pratfall. The smile on his face was gone. His eyes stared up at the sky, unmoving. Emma poked him in the side with her foot. He still didn't move. She used her foot to move his head. It rolled over loosely and she saw his coloured hair was dark and wet. A blunt edge of a rock showing through the leaves. It was bloodied.

"Oh, fuck," she whispered as the evening rain began to fall.

Chapter Two

When Emma was eleven, she went to the circus for the first time. The tent was in a field and it should have looked bright and exciting but years of wear and tear had worn the colours away to shades of beige and washed-out blood. The sky overhead that day had looked empty and her heart felt the same though she didn't know why.

Emma watched the people ahead walking in through the dark fluttering rectangle of the entrance; seeming to disappear for good into the tent's dark interior. Her small hand tightened its grip on Mum's fingers so much that she stopped to ask if Emma was okay.

Emma wanted to be brave so she said yes.

Yes. I'm okay, Mum.

She wasn't, not at all, because there was a smell of manure and sweat, and something else; something she was too young to name. It was in there; a part of the dark inside the tent. She didn't want to see it, meet it, shake its hand, or watch it smile. She knew the smile would be a dead thing and the eyes would be as empty as empty could be – but she went in because she was being brave today.

They sat down on the chairs which surrounded the circus ring. The stuffing was coming out of the cushions on the chairs. The stuffing was pale, tattered and soft. Emma thought it must be made from people who came to the circus; those who didn't make it out again were used to stuff the cushions. She didn't want to sit on one of them but had to. She had to be brave even though she could feel how damp the cushion was, like it was sweating or weeping. Her fingers found their way to the sides of the chair's metal frame, which she gripped hard until her knuckles began to ache.

Horses cantered through the sawdust of the circus ring. A shirtless man who had more fat than muscle on him breathed fire and tried to lift a huge dumb-bell with *10 Tons* flaking off the spherical weights at each end. An old woman with make-up thick as a mask jumped and skipped around tiredly in a leotard as faded as the colours of the circus tent. None of them scared Emma. They just made her feel a bit sad.

The something she was too young to name was coming though. She could smell its wetness and taste its badness in her mouth each time she breathed in. Her fingers hurt a lot from how hard she was gripping the sides of her chair but she didn't let go. She wouldn't let go until it was all over.

The circus ring was empty. The crowd was talking over the silence. Emma gnawed at the inside of her mouth and kicked her trainers' heels against the ground. Mum told her not to do that because it wasn't nice so she stopped, but she kept on biting at the flesh of her cheeks. Whatever was coming next, it was going to be awful.

The clowns came out; shuffling, jumping, bouncing, and rolling. Emma bit at the inside of her mouth so hard she tasted blood. She kept quiet despite the pain as she didn't want the clowns to know they'd scared her. She didn't want them to smell the blood either.

There were three clowns. Their faces were plaster-white, their lips were red, and their eyes were painted black and badged with false tears. They all wore conical, buttoned hats on their heads, and their clothes were elegant patchwork suits with ruffs around their necks and their fingers were dressed in neat, white gloves. They stopped in the centre of the ring and bowed their heads. The crowd was quiet, expectant, waiting.

Emma wanted to go home.

Then, one clown fell to his knees as if he'd been shot, collapsing forwards onto his hands. The second leaned over him; a coroner weeping painted tears, and the third pushed the second hard in the back. The smile of the third was a livid wound. Emma knew he'd shot the first clown. He was the murderer.

The second tumbled, rolled, and sprang back to his feet as the first rose from the dead. The first and second turned on the third with outstretched hands, grasping at the air, seeking for his throat. They were all murderers. Every clown was a killer. She knew that now. They grabbed the third's arms and pulled hard at them. Emma wanted to close her eyes. She didn't want to see them pull his arms off – there would be a lot of blood if they did that – but instead the two clowns fell back as the third flew into the air, tumbled over them, rolled in the sawdust, came back to his feet, and was answered by applause.

Mum was laughing – *why didn't she understand?*

These clowns thought pain was funny; that dying was a joke. Emma looked around and saw other people were laughing too. This was all wrong – but the clowns hadn't finished. A long wooden box was wheeled out on a gurney into the centre of the circus ring. It looked like a coffin to Emma, despite the smiling faces and silver stars painted on it. The clowns spun the box around, rapped at it with their knuckles, shouted into the holes at either end before turning to the crowd to collect the laughter they were due. The clowns opened the box and started talking to the crowd. Their voices were normal; human ones which shouldn't have been coming from faces like that.

The clowns wanted someone to get in the box.

They wanted a child.

Emma did not move. She held her breath. If they smelled the blood in her mouth, they would want to put her in the box. She knew it. Her arms were aching fiercely from how hard she was holding onto the sides of the chair but she didn't care. It was all she could do to stop herself from running away. If she ran then they would catch her and put her in the box. She had to stay quiet. She had to stay still.

Emma closed her eyes and made a wish.

Please-dont-pick-me.

There was a cheer from the crowd.

Emma opened her eyes and looked up. There was a girl standing in the circle with the clowns. A girl who looked a lot like Emma. She had red hair cut short, wore glasses, jeans and a *Thundercats* t-shirt. The girl was smiling. The clowns helped the girl climb into the box. Emma wanted to get up, to scream and shout; to tell her not to do it but she couldn't because then there'd hear her. They would know they had the wrong Emma even though this Emma *was* her, somehow.

The clowns closed the box over the other Emma whilst Emma listened to the beating of her own heart, feeling it as if the box had closed over her. She watched the girl's head and feet sticking out of each end. This other Emma was a toy to them; a plaything they could do with as they pleased.

The first clown pressed a flopping finger to its lips, shushing the crowd. The second pulled off the other Emma's trainers. The third tickled her bare feet. The girl cried out and kicked. The crowd laughed. Emma didn't laugh. The trainers had been the same as hers; grey and battered with little Velcro straps. None of this was funny. She hated having her feet touched, or tickled, too.

The other Emma was still in the box and Emma felt like she couldn't breathe but the pain in her hands and arms anchored her. She was sitting on this chair next to Mum. She wasn't in the box and couldn't be. The third clown brought out a saw, which it flexed in the air so everyone could see its teeth and how big it was. The red wound of the smile on its face was what Emma hated most of all. This one looked like it was enjoying itself far too much. The first and second clowns bowed to the third and moved away from the box, turned to the crowd, and raised their hands in the air. The fingers began to count down in time with shouts from the crowd.

Five ... four ... three ... two ... one ...

The third began to saw through the box. The crowd hushed and the only sound Emma could hear and feel was the serrated teeth passing back and forth through the wood of the box. She waited, aching inside, for the sound to change as the saw bit into flesh and bone. She waited for screams. She waited for the other Emma to die.

The sacrifice made to these painted things which laughed at pain and danced after death.

Come on, come on, come on.

There was no change in the sound of the saw. There was no blood in the sawdust of the circus ring. The act ended. The box opened. The other Emma was okay. Everyone cheered and applauded, except Emma – because she knew the truth. The clowns were hiding in plain sight; showing everyone what they wanted to do to her.

One day, she thought, they'll do it. They'll come after me.

They won't be able to stop themselves.

The sacrifice will be made.

Chapter Three

Emma looked down at the dead man and knew she couldn't leave him like this. He wasn't a clown anymore. He wasn't anything anymore. She dialled 999 on her phone.

"Which emergency service please?"

"Ambulance ... police ... *both!"*

"Which emergency service please?"

"Police ... just police."

"Thank you, putting you through now."

There was a pause and a click on the line.

"Hello, where are you calling from?"

I just killed a man.

"Hello, what is the nature of the emergency?"

It was an accident.

"Is anyone hurt or injured?"

"He's dead ..." Emma whispered, "he's just dead ..."

She turned away from the body. She couldn't look at it.

"Hello? Where are you? Are you hurt?"

Emma hung up. She didn't know why. The words were numb in her mouth.

He's dead. It was an accident. I killed him. I didn't mean to.

"Shit, shit, shit."

She'd ruined everything, made things much worse rather than better. The path ahead was suddenly dark and certain; questions, cold rooms, no answers, hard faces, arrest, court, prison – and yet more punishment. She wasn't sure she could handle more.

No more please.

Emma turned around and saw the evening rain was falling on a bare patch of soil and leaves. The body was gone. She leaned forward and looked at the stone, which had been thickly stained with blood. It was clean – or had it been clean all along?

Had he been there?

"Am I seeing things?"

After the words were said, she smiled. A genuine, pure smile.

He's not dead. Whatever happened, there's no dead body here. I'm okay. We're going to be okay.

"Everything's okay. Mummy's going to be okay." Emma said to Jacob and Liam. She knew that they couldn't hear her but some things needed to be said out loud. Emma began to walk home, wincing at shooting pains in her leg. There was some wine in the fridge. She'd have a glass, maybe two, when she got back then go to bed, sleep it off, and start again tomorrow.

*

Evening was turning to night, making the world a duller place as Emma went on her way. She ignored the language of the leaves as her feet disturbed them and sang her own private, wordless songs over the sound of the wind. She paid no mind to the heavier fall of the rain; and how it sounded like careful footsteps being made amongst the trees. Home wasn't far away, nearly there now.

A white shape moved amongst the trees ahead. Emma ignored it. She kept her thoughts on home and the wine waiting for her. The white shape was not something she welcomed as she seemed to see it passing from tree to tree. Someone's washing, it must be. A bedsheet blown away by the wind, caught up in the branches and flapping about a bit, that's all. It fell onto the path before her and lay there; crumpled, torn, and obstructing the way. Emma made to walk around it.

The white shape bulged upright. Small hands reached out of it, snatching at her. Emma pulled away. The hands cast off the white shape, which was a dirty sheet, and there was a boy standing there. His face was scratched and his blonde hair was ragged.

"Jake?"

Could it be him?

Pale-faced and dressed in a minute clown suit of red, blue and white stripes. No, he was with Grandma and Grandad and this boy was different somehow. His little face was painted with black cross-hatched eyes and his lips were painted blue as frostbite – except Emma felt certain that if she touched his face, tried to wipe the make-up away, she would find it was one with his skin. This couldn't be Jacob.

"What are you doing here?" she asked, refusing to say his name.

She edged closer to him as she spoke, wanting this boy to be someone else. She had to see him up close without the obscuring shadows of twilight. She had to know.

"Mummy?"

It was his voice. No, it couldn't be. His eyes didn't blink as he looked at her and he was standing very still. Jacob blinked a lot and fidgeted too.

"They're coming for you, Mummy."

"Who are? Who's coming?"

It looked like him. It sounded like him.

"They're coming for you, Mummy. It's time for it to happen."

"Time for what?"

"The sacrifice, Mummy. It has to be tonight."

He was close enough to touch. She had to touch him and know.

"You can't run from them, Mummy, because they're bad things and bad things always come back." He smiled as he said this. It was the smile of a clown not her little boy. Emma reached out. Her fingers fastened on the clown suit and she pulled hard at it – and he was gone. Sticks tied into little bundles fell to the ground. A paper-plate mask rolled into the bushes. The clown suit hung empty in her hands. Emma threw the thing away then went and stamped on it with her foot.

Good foot. Bad leg. More pain. Shit.

Emma ground the small clown suit into the dirt and then looked around. There were no more shape moving in the trees. She took out her phone and dialled. Rain fell on the smartphone screen, making it slip under her fingers as the numbers blurred. There wasn't much of evening left and she wasn't out of the woods yet but she had to do this now. She had to know. The line rang, rang and rang.

Grandma picked up.

"Hi, Rose. Is Jakey there? Is he okay?"

"Of course, he is," came the reply, "He's fine, dear."

"Have they been watching films?" she had to say something, make the call sound normal.

"Oh yes, quite a few today. The weather here's taken a turn for the worst so no playing outside."

"What've they been watching?"

"Old stuff with Grandad. Something with clowns, I think. You want me to put them on?"

"No, it's okay. It's nothing, just … nothing, nothing. Don't worry. I was just being … silly. I missed them."

"Ah, don't you worry yourself about missing them. It's fine, dear. Happened to me when I was your age, back when your Mum was a babe. We're taking good care of them. You just have yourself a nice time on your own and you'll see them soon."

"Yeah, I will. I'll try to. Thanks, Rose."

"You take care now, love."

"You too, Rose."

"You take care, dear. G'night."

Grandma hung up, leaving Emma standing in the woods and wondering what she was going to do. She hadn't asked Rose to call the police. She should have done. Something was up here. He could still be out there; the man in the clown-suit, wanting revenge.

They're coming, Mummy.

She dialled 999 once more.

This time, the line was dead.

Chapter Four

Emma tried to sleep after she saw the clowns at the circus but couldn't. She was too big for a night-light and she wouldn't have asked for one anyway. She had to be brave and not let the clowns scare her. The house around her was asleep and, like the comfort of an ageing relative, it sighed and moaned as it settled. Like an old tree in autumn, it creaked itself steadily to rest. The clock beside the bed told Emma it was almost three o'clock. Mum had told her stories about this time of night; it was the witching hour when the scary things were at their strongest.

There were eyes watching her. She could feel them. They were touching her – how could watching eyes touch though? They could because they could; the feeling of being looked at until it's like fingers touching your skin.

There were always eyes watching her in the house. Mum collected porcelain dolls and they could be found in every room. Wherever there was a space, Mum put a doll. They watched the days and nights pass by with their unseeing eyes, half-smiling as if they knew something blackly amusing.

Nights when she needed to get up to pee were the worst ones for Emma. The toilet was downstairs under the stairs which meant leaving her room and having to face the dolls. At this time of night, when the house was buried in shadows, few of the dolls could be seen clearly but she knew they were there; on the bookshelves, in corners, behind the closed doors, peeping out through curtains. As she padded barefoot through the house, a polished profile might come into view, a round, white face could find its way out of the dimness, or a spotless hand would reach out for her with its moulded fingers. Emma hurried past them all; her breath, heart and footsteps all beating in time. The house was not her house after dark, it was *their* house and, perhaps, that was why they smiled the way they did – and tonight was a night when she had to pee.

The dolls were waiting but she knew if she were quick then she'd not be too scared. Taking a deep breath, Emma threw back the bedcovers and fumbled at the floor with her toes for a moment as the uneasiness of half-sleep retreated. The door of her room looked like it was made from the same porcelain as the dolls with the light of moon on it. The handle felt as cold as porcelain as well when Emma touched it and turned it around until she heard the click.

There was a creak like footsteps and a sigh like someone's breath as she opened the bedroom door. Emma decided she had made the sounds. Dolls didn't move or breathe, they only watched – and that was enough. She closed the door behind her and saw the hallway before her as a tunnel cut from night-loam. Dismembered light was scattered across the floor; having passed through curtains, seeped through window-cracks, and crept around doors. Emma could see only pieces of the house as she knew it by day and, as she heard the house settle itself earlier, she was sure that now she could hear sounds of something else waking up. The dolls, of course. She knew they were there, but could there also be something even the dolls were afraid of?

Emma padded through the stuttering dark-light, light-dark of the hallway until she reached the top of the stairs and began to make her way down. She took one step at a time, holding onto the bannister with both hands. She was big enough to use one but the house made her feel small at this time of night so she descended like a child half her age. Shadows fell across the stairs in ways that argued and conflicted, and she could never tell if one of them wasn't going to reach out and give her a push; a little push by a cold, little hand shaped from porcelain.

She reached the bottom of the stairs and turned, as always, to look back up the stairs. Vertigo washed over her as the top of the stairs looked like a mouth of swallowing darkness. She looked away from it.

Emma padded around to the toilet under the stairs, opened the door, and reached for the cord to turn on the light. She pulled the cord and the light came on. The bulb cracked and the light went out. In the moment where there was light, Emma saw something was there. It had been one of Mum's dolls with a smooth face, glassy eyes and wry smile but dressed up as one of the clowns from the circus. Mum had said they were called Pierrot – but there were no dolls in the house that looked like those clowns.

And its eyes had been made of something which was *not* glass.

Emma reached out to slam the toilet door shut but a shape came at her in the dark; a puppet lunging forward on its loose yet unforgiving strings. She heard the *thump-thump* of small, hard feet. She felt cold porcelain touching her cold skin. Emma screamed. Her bravery was gone – a collapsed shrunken and powerless thing. Utterly spent. Her voice filled the void of the house until she felt empty herself.

Lights came on and washed away the shadows as Mum, awake, came pounding down the stairs and wrapped the girl Emma had been up in her arms. She buried herself deep in Mum's embrace; drinking in the scent of rose perfume and stale cigarettes.

Eventually, she calmed down and Mum let her go but, before going back up the overlit stairs to bed, Emma turned to look for the clown doll. It wasn't there – though there were small, faint impressions in the carpet which could've been footprints. They would be gone by morning but, wherever he'd gone, he'd be coming back for her.

Chapter Five

Emma followed the path into the dark of the woods, using her phone's screen-light as a make-shift torch. She hadn't tried calling anyone else. Whoever picked up, she had a feeling that she wouldn't like what she heard. It was cold in the woods. The rain had eased but the tangle of trees seemed like it was in on whatever was happening as it was not letting her go. Her trainers were soaked through and her socks squelched unpleasantly with each step. Home was nowhere in sight, only the black of the trees cast against the black of night lay before her. Her bad leg ached from the cold and, for the hundredth time, she thought about how she'd like the surgeon who'd done this to her to die slowly. I just want to go home, Emma thought miserably as she slogged onwards, why can't I find my way?

There!

A light in the trees, burning softly. She began to jog towards it, praying for a pub or something similar by the motorway. She could orient herself then and find her way home. Her leg complained of the jogging after a short while and she dropped back to a brisk walking pace. The light passed back and forth between the trees as she came closer to it. Thankfully, it didn't dim, go out, or become lost in the bracken. It led her out into another open part of the woods and she saw the last remains of a church standing before her.

The light burned from inside a singular window of a half-fallen wall like a watchful eye. Its glow made the shadows lengthen and draw themselves in around her like long fingers sifting through the undergrowth. She could hear voices inside the ruin; low and sonorous. She moved carefully so as not to be heard, not trusting whoever might be out in the woods at this hour. Today had not been a good day for meeting strangers.

Emma drew closer to the light and saw a cluster of figures gathered in the church's broken heart. She caught glimpses as the light played over them and felt her mouth dry up altogether. There were beggar clowns, derelict harlequins, and haggard mimes standing in a shuffling, uneven circle. They swayed as the clown she'd met in the clearing had swayed though this time the words they were chanting explained the rhythm.

"Ekkeri, akai-ri, u kair-an! Fillissin, follasy, nakelas ja'n!"

She had no idea what the words meant, but the solemn tone of the clowns' voices suggested ritual.

The sacrifice will be made.

As Emma watched through the church's remaining window, she saw a clown emerge from the gloom, leading a much smaller figure by the hand. The clown was unlike the others; neat and clean with a spotless, alabaster face. Each eye was marked by a single black teardrop painted beneath and his rouge lips were a livid wound, like the third clown she had seen at the circus on that day so many years ago.

Was this creature *her* Pierrot?

The smaller figure was a young boy. He was nude and must've been about Liam's age. His hair was the same tousled mess. The boy's face was turned away from her. Some part of her wanted to cry out Liam's name but she she stayed where she was. She felt her fingers clenching as she watched the scene unfold. The fingernails digging into her palms until she could feel them pressing on tendon and bone.

The Pierrot led the child towards the gathering of clowns. They parted and Emma saw the altar which had been concealed by their bodies before. It was crude and henge-like with four uncarved rocks supporting an altar stone partially-cracked lengthways. The Pierrot directed the boy to the altar. Emma could see the boy's skinny, bare legs trembling as he climbed gingerly onto the cold stone.

The chanting of the clowns intensified.

"Ekkeri, akai-ri, u kair-an! Ekkeri, akai-ri, u kair-an!"

The Pierrot snapped his gloved fingers at the gathering of clowns and four of his kin came forward. Each of the four took a wrist or ankle so that the boy was spread-eagle on the altar. The boy was quiet and Emma wondered why; what'd been done to make him so acquiescent to the Pierrot's will? She decided that she didn't want to know.

The Pierrot clapped his hands together and the chanting of the clowns ceased. He stood behind the altar and made a sweeping gesture towards the pinioned boy, *"Chiv o manzin apre lati!"*

The clowns surged towards the altar as a murmuring mass with their hands outstretched. From where she was, Emma could see over the heads of the gathering so the altar was not obscured as they clustered around it but what she saw made her wish she had not. The fingers of the clowns went roaming over the boy's torso like pale, dirty spiders. The way they touched his small body, the way they stroked, fondled, and pinched at his skin made her feel sick. She could see the boy's face and it was not Liam. A part of her which she might have hated was grateful.

The boy's face was streaked with tears as his voice rose in a cry and took on the quality of something fragile breaking, something innocent being irredeemably lost. There was laughter when they tickled him as a thin, desperate sound – threaded through with tears and a longing to get away from these creatures. Each touch they made was a form of taking. Each caress of their fingers was wearing away at something more precious than his nerves. The Pierrot stood aside as a voyeur for the most part, until he decided to reach down, pinch and tweak one of the boy's nipples with his immaculate gloved fingers.

Emma couldn't stand it a moment longer. She clambered through the window and ran towards the crowd of clowns. She pushed through them; elbowing, shoving and kicking. They felt ripe and rotten. They reeked of wetness and manure. They let her through, falling away, soft as scarecrows, with nothing but a dull confusion showing in their eyes. She shouldered the last clown aside and stood at the altar, face to face with the Pierrot. He met her gaze calmly. The altar was between them and, despite herself, Emma was glad of it. The Pierrot's eyes were ancient torture-holes which shone with a queer animate light. His painted flesh looked clammy and hard as death, like cold porcelain. The stitching on his suit shimmered like northern aurorae. Emma did not flinch away from his eyes though it felt like they were peering deep inside her, seeking something out. Without thinking, she placed her hand on the chest of the boy and said, "This one's mine. Let him go. Let him be."

The Pierrot's eyes flickered for a moment then he raised his hands and gently clapped twice. He cast his eyes at each clown holding the boy down, and each clown retreated in turn, letting the child go. The boy shrank in on himself, curling foetal. He sobbed quietly on the altar with his arms tight around his bony knees.

Emma snatched up the boy, keeping her eyes on the Pierrot as she backed away from the altar. She felt the clowns parting at her back, letting her through. The Pierrot watched her go; a calmness rested in his eyes which she did not like.

She ran out of the church ruin and into the woods as the light within went out soundlessly. She ran as far as she could for as long as she could before her bad leg began its searing protest of pins, needles, and pain. She ground her teeth against the spasming of the muscles until her leg gave out and they both sprawled into a low bank of dead leaves. She got to her knees and her whole body trembled with her leg as its pain brought tears to her eyes which she blinked fiercely away. There was no time for weeping.

The boy squatted on the ground before her; whining in his throat and scratching his fingertips through the top soil of the mulchy ground. Emma looked him in the eye. He was chewing at his lips, making them sore and bloody. He'd probably gnawed a few holes into the inside of his mouth as well. Each breath he let out was a keen whistling sound. Emma, short of breath, pointed through the trees, away towards the boundaries where there would be light, traffic, and people. "Go. Run for it. That way. Find someone. Get help."

The boy stopped scratching at the ground and followed her finger with his eyes into the outer dark of the woods. He turned his reddened eyes back to her and shook his head, whining in his throat again.

"You must," Emma gasped, "they're in the trees. They're coming. Don't let them take you again. You musn't go back."

The boy reached out a frail, trembling hand and she took it, squeezing it hard. She tried to smile but it was hard. The boy said two quiet words, "Thank you."

"Find someone," she said, "go."

He scrambled to his feet and ran. Emma watched him run; a small ghost vanishing into the dark and thought how true it was – that's all we're looking for really – to find someone to help us, to share life with; the hurt, the pain, and the world's constant cruelty. Another soul as well as your own to help you survive each day a little better.

She knew her boys were safe and now this boy was safe. In the short time she'd held him in her arms, she'd cared no less for him than if he'd been one of her own children.

Only a mother can heal a child.

Branches rustled and dead leaves crackled. The clowns were coming. She had to run as in a childhood fairy-tale, all the way home; dashing through shadows, passing by fear, with her nerves burning and her bad leg slowing her down.

Emma knew one thing though. They would not be following the boy. She'd seen recognition in the Pierrot's shining eyes. He wanted her much more than the boy. She'd denied him twice as a child and he remembered this well.

They were coming for her alone.

Chapter Six

Emma made it home.

The woods let her go free; parting like black wings so that she found herself staggering along the narrow path up the incline and then between the houses and back onto her street. Ageing cars rested in front of red, homogenised blocks of terraced housing. The sodium streetlights stuttered on and off. She could hear the raised voices of families and see the bright rhythm of television outlining curtains drawn across living room windows.

Home was a dozen feet away, just across the street – it didn't seem possible.

She'd be there and safe in a minute. A quick call to the police that she'd been chased by someone threatening to break into her home and assault her, and it would be over. She had an idea that the blue lights of a police car would banish the Pierrot completely and turn him into the dust of forgotten dreams. Some things could not co-exist.

Emma looked back down the sloping path into the woods and saw only fallen leaves hurrying over the marks of her footsteps. She got her breath back by increments and the pulse of her heart slowly stopped labouring with the pain in her leg. She crossed the street, dug out her door keys and let herself in.

She plucked the handset out of its cradle mounted on the hallway wall and dialled 999 for the fourth time that night. As the tone rang in her ears, she wiped the grease of settled sweat from her forehead and ran fingers through her dishevelled hair. A shower would be a good idea before bed.

The tone cut off as someone came on the line.

"Hello? Can I have police, please?"

Nothing but the sound of someone's light, unsteady breathing.

"Hello? Who's there?" Emma said, feeling her voice growing thin.

The breathing changed to a quiet sobbing and she swallowed any words she might've spoken. The sobbing became harsh, hitching moans and, between them, she heard the boy from the woods, *"Thank you."*

The boy's last words were lost as a series of cries were violently torn from his throat; piercing Emma's ears with their ferocity. There came a point where they were less cries and more the sustained white noise of a child's distress. She only realised the line had gone dead when the ringing in her ears was all that remained of the boy's voice.

She slumped to the floor in the hallway with the handset hanging limply from her fingers.

There was nothing coming from it but the whining of a dead line. Emma's eyes looked at a point in the distance beyond the walls of the house, beyond the woods, which was buried somewhere deep inside of herself as well.

The Pierrot had lied, or had she lied to herself?

The boy was gone. Lost to darkness. She'd lost him. It was her fault.

Hope was a mistake; a lie told from mother to child.

She didn't look up as the Pierrot came softly down the stairs; black-eyed and smiling. He offered her his hand and Emma took it. She followed him back up the stairs. There was glass on the floor from where he'd broken all of the lightbulbs on the first floor. Emma's trainers trod the shards into the carpet. They were waiting for her in the bedroom, all of the clowns were there; patient and quiet as they stood around the bed muttering their ritual words.

"Ekkeri, akai-ri, u kair-an! Fillissin, follasy, nakelas ja'n!"

The Pierrot led her in as he'd led the boy to the altar. He led her as she had been led ever since she first saw him in the circus tent, smiling and waving at the crowd, seeking for sure prey with his blackly shining eyes. Emma lay down on the bed without a word and looked up at the ceiling, at the patterns of dismembered light there and saw no sense in them at all; no rhyme, no reason – only darkness and loss. There was no path left for her to follow. All was nothing and nothing was all.

"*Ekkeri, akai-ri, u kair-an! Ekkeri, akai-ri, u kair-an!*"

The Pierrot drew the curtains across the bedroom window, shutting out the last of the light. The room closed in around her as an absolute shadow and breath caught in her throat as she felt hard panels of wood appearing to trap her on all sides. Emma let her breath go, closed her eyes and the reopened them. There was light of a sort seeping in from somewhere; it came down through tears in a striped, fluctuating awning far above. She was no longer in her bedroom. There were stars showing in the night sky visible through the tears, but they were not stars which she'd ever seen before.

Emma turned her head from side to side. A number of familiar things began to form themselves from the strange starlight; the faces of an audience, slack and dun-coloured, worn into silence by decades of waiting; the wooden circle of a circus ring with its bright colours long since peeled away, and the dust scattered across the ground glimmered queerly; there was Mum, as she had once been, holding hands with a child in the adjoining seat. The child was not dressed in jeans and a *Thundercats* t-shirt. Its eyes shone as if it were wearing glasses though Emma was not sure there were eyes underneath. The skin of the child had the same damp, uneven texture as the stuffing which leaked from the cushions. It sat so calmly and Mum looked so placidly happy as if this were the daughter she'd wanted Emma to be.

Emma was in the box at the centre of the circus ring; the one she'd been promised to at eleven years of age. She could not move. Her head and feet were the only parts of her body outside of the box. The air in this circus tent was old and cold and made her want to hold her breath. She withstood the removal of her trainers and socks without protest, and the rags of unkept fingernails stroking against the bare soles of her feet. The clowns were restless. They wanted that which had been promised to them.

The Pierrot raised and clapped his hands. *"Chiv o manzin apre lati!"*

There was a rustling from the audience; it might have been what was left of their voices, or the sound of their dry hands applauding – and then the clowns were upon her. Their eyes were dead moons and the touch of their fingers – so many fingers – tortured her. Emma's laughter turned to tears and to cries as her knees jerked away from them and banged against the topmost panel of the box. Pain sang through her limbs but faded s the feeling of the clowns scratching and stroking at her feet and ankles returned. She closed her eyes tight as a few of them began to suckle wetly on her toes.

As time went on, her cries were worn down to croaks and then to a dry, choking sound which rustled and scraped against the back of her throat. Her elbows and hands rapped hard against the rough interior of the box but did no more than spread further traces of pain throughout her body.

She passed out at times – awoke to shadows blurring together whilst everything else whistled and sang – gasping from a fear of swallowing and gagging on her tongue. The one constant was the clowns; their excruciating touch and their distant, glimmering eyes. For here she was, bound by reality – laughing alongwith its joyless laughter and feeling all of its empty, unending pain. When the clowns brought out the saw, she barely felt its teeth pass through the enclosing wood, then her flesh, and then her bones. There was no blood though there should have been plenty to stain the dusty ground. She listened to the sound of small unoiled wheels as the lower half of the box was dragged away into shadows outside of the circus ring, leaving the rest of her behind. Emma thought she caught glimpses of pale limbs, hanging and twitching, in that lost darkness – and so many more clowns milling about in the shadows. They were plucking, stroking, and suckling at those dangling, wan remains, which were disembodied yet still somehow alive. Would she hang alongside them in time; another broken marionette strung from the hidden rafters of a forgotten cosmic attic born outside the universe?

Emma could still feel her legs, what was being done to them, and wished that she could not. There was no mercy here. Consciousness and unconsciousness tasted much the same on her aching tongue. Her suffering had grown steadily to fill the unclear void within the funereal circus, as her voice and the voices of her boys once filled the home they shared. Jacob and Liam; they would learn the truth of things one day – but not just yet. Bad things always come back, but not always to the same people. She wanted the boys here so she could tell them that. They were not here so she did what she could to stop such a day as this coming to pass for them. Emma looked and found the hollow-bright eyes of the Pierrot clown. He was standing over her, watching as always, and she made unto him a prayer; *Let me have it. Please. Let all the pain be for me. Do it to me and not to them. If this must be forever then let it be, just leave my boys alone. Let them be.*

The clown smiled, gently stroked a stray, sweat-beaded hair from her forehead, and pressed an immaculate, gloved finger to his lips;

•

and silence followed in that faraway circus, with no applause. Fade to black.

End

Author's Note

Thank you for reading **The Clowns Outside**. I hope you enjoyed it. If you have a moment, I would also greatly appreciate it if you left a review on the site where you purchased this ebook. No matter how big or small it is, every review counts and matters to a writer because without you, the readers, we are nothing.

About the Author

Greg James is a critically-acclaimed and best-selling self-published author. He was born in Essex and grew up along the south-east coast of England. He studied literature and media at university and has taught English as a foreign language in the Far East. He has written the acclaimed Vetala Cycle series and the best-selling Age of the Flame trilogy. He lives in London where he can be found writing into the small hours of the morning during the week, and sleeping in on Saturdays.